The Incredible Journey

SHEILA BURNFORD

Level 3

Retold by Joanna Strange
Series Editors: Andy Hopkins and Jocelyn Potter

Pearson Education Limited
Edinburgh Gate, Harlow,
Essex CM20 2JE, England
and Associated Companies throughout the world

ISBN 0582 82986 0

First published in Great Britain by Hodder and Stoughton Limited, 1961
This edition first published by Penguin Books 2004

3 5 7 9 10 8 6 4

Text copyright © Penguin Books 2004
Illustrations © Duncan Smith 2004

Set in 11/14pt Bembo
Printed in Spain by Mateu Cromo, S.A. Pinto, Madrid

Produced for the publishers by Bluestone Press, Charlbury, Oxfordshire, UK

Published by Pearson Education Limited in association with
Penguin Books Ltd., both companies being subsidiaries of Pearson Plc

For a complete list of the titles available in the Penguin Readers series please write to your local
Pearson Education office or to: Marketing Department, Penguin Longman Publishing,
Edinburgh Gate, Harlow, Essex CM20 2JE.

Contents

Introduction

John Longridge returned from his vacation to an empty house. He looked for the animals everywhere: in the house, in the yard, in the fields. He called and called, but there was no answer…

"The animals have disappeared," Longridge said sadly. "But they were happy here. Why did they leave?"

John Longridge is looking after some animals which belong to his good friends, the Hunter family. There is Luath, a proud, young, red-gold Labrador retriever. Then there is Tao, a beautiful, curious Siamese cat. And finally Bodger, a brave, old, white bull terrier.

One beautiful fall day, when Longridge goes on vacation, the animals decide to go home. But home is 400 kilometers away! And the journey is through wild, dangerous country. The three friends struggle through lonely forests, with very little food. Exhausted and weak, they fight for their lives against wild animals. They swim across fast, deep rivers and sleep outside in the cold and dark.

Will the animals escape death on this dangerous journey? Will they ever reach home safely and see their family again?

How will their incredible journey end?

Sheila Burnford was born in Scotland in 1918. She and her husband had three children and three family pets. The idea for *The Incredible Journey*, her first book, came from these pets. The story takes place in Canada, in the northwest of Ontario. Disney made the book into a popular movie in 1963 (in black and white), and thirty years later with the title *Homeward Bound: The Incredible Journey* (in color).

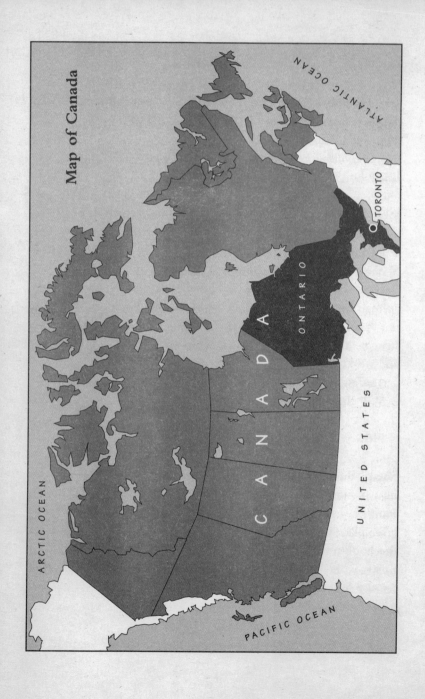

Map of Canada

Chapter 1 The Three Friends

The journey took place in Canada, in the northwest of Ontario. This part of the country is wild, with woods, lakes, and fast rivers. There are thousands of kilometers of narrow country roads, a few small towns, and lonely farms. Men from the big paper companies cut down trees deep in the forests. There are Indians and hunters. But most of the time there are no human beings, only wild animals. And silence.

For almost half the year the area is covered in snow, and the temperature falls below zero for weeks. The seasons are different in north Ontario. The plants and flowers do not grow slowly in spring. There is a sudden, short summer when everything grows fast. Then it is fall again with clear blue skies, sunny days, and wonderful, richly colored leaves on the trees: gold and yellow and red.

Through this wild, lonely country, in the fall, the three travelers made their incredible journey.

♦

John Longridge lived alone a long way from one of the small towns, in an old stone house that belonged to his family. He was a tall man of about forty, serious but kind. He was a writer of history books and traveled a lot. But he always returned to the comfortable old stone house to write his books. Mrs. Oakes and her husband Bert lived about a kilometer away. Mrs. Oakes went to Longridge's home every day. She looked after the house and cooked his main meals. Bert looked after the backyard. They understood Longridge very well. While he was writing, they worked quietly around the place.

On the evening before the incredible journey, toward the end of September, Longridge was reading a newspaper by a warm wood fire in his comfortable library. He couldn't turn the pages easily because a Siamese cat with bright blue eyes was sitting on his knees. From time to time, the cat moved his brown front paws as he looked into the fire.

On the floor, with his head on one of Longridge's feet, lay an old white bull terrier. His eyes were closed and his tail moved in his sleep. Some people think bull terriers are strange, ugly dogs. But Longridge loved him: he was a friendly family pet and, at the same time, a strong, brave fighter. The man always enjoyed the look of happiness in the old dog's little eyes.

By the door lay another dog with his nose on his paws. This was a large red–gold Labrador retriever, a young dog with a strong body. His brown eyes were wide open, watching everything. When Longridge got up from his chair, the dog lifted his proud head.

Longridge put the cat on the floor and carefully moved his foot from under the old dog's head. He walked across the room and looked out the window. A huge orange moon was coming up just above the trees at the far end of the yard. It was bright outside from the light of the moon. Longridge could see the leaves on the grass. There were a few colorful flowers, still there from the summer.

He turned, crossed the room, and turned on another light. Next he opened a narrow cupboard halfway up the wall. Inside were a lot of guns. He took one out and looked at it carefully. The Labrador sat up when he saw the gun. He looked at it with excitement and great interest. When Longridge put the gun back in the cupboard, the young dog lay down again. He turned his head away, his eyes unhappy.

Suddenly, the telephone rang and broke the silence of the quiet room. Woken by the noise, the cat jumped angrily off the chair. The old bull terrier struggled to his feet. Longridge answered the phone. He could hear Mrs. Oakes, but her voice was not very clear.

"Speak louder, Mrs. Oakes," he said. "I can't hear you."

"I can't hear you very well either," said Mrs. Oakes. "Is that better? I'm shouting now! What time are you leaving in the morning, Mr. Longridge? Excuse me? Could you talk louder please?"

"About seven o'clock. I want to get to Heron Lake before dark," he shouted. "But you don't have to be here at that time, Mrs. Oakes."

"What did you say? Seven? Will it be all right if I come at about nine? My daughter's arriving on the early bus and I'd like to meet her. But I don't want to leave the dogs alone too long…"

"Of course you must meet her," John shouted. "The dogs will be fine. I'll take them out before I leave and…"

"Oh, thank you, Mr. Longridge. I'll be there at about nine, I promise. What did you say about the animals? Don't worry about them. Bert and I will…"

But Longridge couldn't hear her. He put down the phone, walked over to the outside door, and opened it wide. The three animals followed him and ran out into the cold night air. Longridge stood at the door, quietly smoking his pipe. The animals did the same thing every night. For the first few minutes they stayed in the yard, then they all ran into the fields. As they disappeared into the darkness (the old bull terrier far behind the other two), Longridge turned back into the house.

♦

Longridge and his brother owned a cabin on Heron Lake, over three hundred kilometers away. Twice a year they went there together for two or three weeks to fish and hunt. Mrs. Oakes and Bert looked after the house and the three animals while Longridge was away on vacation. Bert worked in the yard, so the animals could be outside most of the time. Mrs. Oakes fed them while she was working in the house.

Longridge finished packing and went into the library. He sat down and wrote a note.

Dear Mrs. Oakes, he wrote, *I've taken some coffee and sugar with me. Please buy some more. I will take the dogs (and the cat too, of course!)…*

Here he came to the end of the small square of paper. He took another piece and continued:

…out for a run before I leave. I will give them something to eat too. Don't worry about them. I know they will be fine with you and Bert.

He left the note on the desk, then opened the outside door. The old dog and the cat hurried in to greet him. They brought the fresh smell of the fields with them. The young dog followed behind, walking calmly. The old dog wagged his tail against Longridge's legs. The cat pressed against him too. He moved his tail politely from side to side when the man softly touched him. The Labrador stood near them and watched quietly.

The cat then walked into the library to lie down in front of the warm fire. Every night he lay there first, and later moved upstairs to Longridge's bed. The cat could go everywhere in the house because he could open all the doors himself!

The young dog walked over to his bed on the kitchen floor, and the bull terrier started climbing up the stairs to Longridge's bedroom. Longridge followed him, undressed, and got into bed. But he couldn't sleep. He lay awake and thought about his trip the next day, and about the animals. He was unhappy about the sad look in the young dog's eyes. He really didn't want to leave them all alone when he went away.

◆

The three strange, lovable animals belonged to the family of an old and dear college friend. This friend, Jim Hunter, was a professor of English in a small college about four hundred kilometers away. Longridge often stayed with him, his wife, and their two children, Elizabeth and Peter.

The three strange, lovable animals belonged to the family of an old and dear college friend.

When the professor was invited to teach at a college in England for nine months, Elizabeth and Peter wanted to go with their parents. But they couldn't take their pets. Longridge could see that the children were very unhappy about the animals. He loved Elizabeth and Peter and he could understand their feelings.

The cat, Tao, belonged to nine-year-old Elizabeth. She looked after him, fed him, took him for walks, and he slept at the bottom of her bed. Eleven-year-old Peter couldn't remember a day in his life without Bodger, the terrier, a gift to him on his first birthday. The Labrador, Luath, belonged to their father. The young dog often went hunting with his master.

Longridge sat and watched the family. Everybody was very quiet, thinking about the animals. Then he suddenly heard a voice, his own voice! "Don't worry," the voice said. "I'll look after the animals while you're in England. I know them well already. And I've got a big house and a large yard. Mrs. Oakes will love them. Everything will be wonderful! Before you leave for England, you can bring them to me. You can see where they'll sleep. And you can give me a list of things that they like to eat. I'll look after them until you come back."

So one day the Hunter family drove to Longridge's house and left their three pets. Elizabeth cried when she had to say goodbye to Tao. Peter gave Longridge a long list of Bodger's needs.

During the first few days the animals looked unhappy and Longridge was worried about them. But soon, with the help of Mrs. Oakes's delicious food, the old terrier and the cat seemed happy and comfortable. They started to love their new master.

Then Bodger started disappearing in the afternoons. Longridge didn't know where he went. Finally, one day, he saw the terrier in the school playground. The dog walked over the fields every afternoon to play with the school children!

But the young Labrador, Luath, was very different. He ate well and looked healthy, but he never stopped missing his home and master. He didn't come close to Longridge like the other two, and he seemed nervous. He was always listening and waiting for something far away. Longridge felt sorry for Luath and worried about him.

◆

Longridge fell asleep at last. Downstairs the dreaming, curious moon shone through the window and woke the cat. He got up, his huge blue eyes wide open, sat near the window, and looked out at the yard. Only his tail moved. Then he turned and jumped onto the desk. One of the pages of Longridge's note to Mrs. Oakes flew into the air. It sailed across the room and landed on the fire. As it slowly burned, the writing disappeared.

The pale light from the moon reached the young dog in the kitchen. He moved uncomfortably in his sleep, then sat up. He was listening for a sound that never came: his master's voice.

Finally the moon lit the upstairs bedroom. There Longridge lay asleep in his bed with the old bull terrier, warm and happy, against his back.

Chapter 2   The Journey Begins

Longridge got up early the next morning. The sun was already shining over the fields and through the bedroom window. It was the beginning of a perfect, warm fall day. He shaved and dressed quickly, and then went downstairs. The animals were waiting patiently by the outside door for their early morning run. He let them out, then cooked and ate his breakfast.

He was putting his bags in the car when the dogs and the cat returned from the fields. He gave them some cookies and they lay by the wall of the house in the sun. They watched him as he put his guns and hunting equipment into the back of the car. When it was time to leave, he crossed the yard to the animals. He said goodbye to each of them.

"Be good. Mrs. Oakes will be here soon. Goodbye, Luath," he said to the Labrador retriever. "I know you want to come with me. I'd like to take you, but I can't. Our boat is too small for three of us."

As he spoke, he put his hand on the young dog's soft face. The golden-brown eyes looked into his, and then the dog did an unusual thing. He lifted his right paw and placed it in the man's hand! Longridge was surprised at the dog's friendliness. "Thank you, Luath," he said. "You're a good friend."

He looked at his watch. "I have to go now," he said to the animals. "I'm already late." He wasn't worried about leaving them alone in the yard. They never went far without him. And when they wanted to get back into the house, they could push the door open. They all looked happy in the sun too. The cat was washing carefully behind his ears. The old dog was resting after his early morning run, with his long pink tongue hanging out of his smiling mouth. And the Labrador lay quietly by the terrier's side.

Longridge started the car, waved to the animals through the window, and drove slowly down the road. He smiled to himself, feeling stupid. "What do I want them to do?" he laughed. "Wave to me? Or shout 'Goodbye'? I've lived alone too long, and I'm beginning to love them too much."

The car turned a corner and disappeared. The cat started washing one of his back legs; the old dog lay down and went to sleep. The young dog stayed near him; only his eyes moved, and his nose from time to time.

Twenty minutes passed. Then suddenly, the young dog got up and looked hard down the road. He stayed like this for a long time. The cat watched him closely, with one leg up in the air. Then the Labrador started to walk slowly down the road. After a few seconds he stopped, turned, and looked back at the others. He was inviting them to follow. The old dog struggled up to his feet and joined him. Together they turned the corner of the road and disappeared from the cat's view.

He stayed by the house for a minute, blue eyes shining in his dark face. Then, with a curious run, he started to follow the two dogs. They were waiting by the gate when he turned the corner. When the cat reached them, the Labrador continued up the road. But the old terrier didn't move. He looked back, hoping to see Mrs. Oakes with some delicious food. And the cat stood next to him, with one paw in the air. He didn't know what to do. Then suddenly, they both decided to follow Luath. Soon all three disappeared down the road, walking quickly and with purpose.

◆

About an hour later, Mrs. Oakes walked up the road. She was carrying a bag with her working clothes and some special food for the animals. "That's strange," she thought. "Where are the dogs? They usually run up to say hello. Maybe Mr. Longridge left them inside the house."

But when she pushed open the kitchen door, there was complete silence. She stood at the bottom of the stairs and called the animals. Nothing happened. Then she walked through the quiet house and out into the front yard. She called again, but they didn't come.

"Maybe they've gone up to the school," she said to herself in the empty, sunny yard. She went back into the kitchen and sat down. "It's funny that Tao isn't here, though," she thought as she put on her work shoes. "He usually sits near the window at this time of day. Maybe he's out hunting again."

She washed and put away some dishes. Then she went into the living room. On the desk she saw Longridge's note. She read the first page. Then she looked for a second piece of paper but couldn't find one.

"That's strange," she thought. "Where has Mr. Longridge taken them? The second page of the note must be here somewhere."

But when she searched the room, she couldn't find anything. Then, when she was cleaning the fireplace, she noticed a burnt piece of paper. She picked it up carefully, but there was no writing on it now.

"That's very strange," she said to herself while she cleaned the room. "In his note he's written, *I will take the dogs (and the cat too of course!).* He's taken the animals to Heron Lake with him! But why has he suddenly done that? He asked me and Bert to look after them. He didn't say anything about it on the telephone last night. But wait a minute! I remember now! He said something about the animals that I couldn't hear. Maybe he was trying to tell me about a new plan."

Mrs. Oakes finished cleaning the house, locked it, and went home. She thought that the animals were traveling north, on vacation with Longridge in the back of his car. She had no idea that they were now on a lonely country road, going west.

♦

For the first hour of their journey the animals moved quite quickly. The bull terrier and the Labrador walked together. The old dog couldn't see out of his left eye, so the Labrador walked near him on his left side. Behind them came the cat. Always curious, he often stopped for a few minutes to look at things. Then he had to run after the dogs. His long, thin body moved quickly along the road with his tail close to the ground.

Soon the old dog got tired, so they turned off the quiet road. They stopped in a wood next to a clear, fast-running stream. The bull terrier was very thirsty and drank deeply. The cat walked over to a rock and sat on it.

Later, they rested in the dry leaves under the trees. The old dog lay, exhausted, with his eyes half closed. The cat was busy washing

She had no idea that they were now on a lonely country road.

himself as usual. After about an hour the young dog got up and started to walk toward the road. The old dog stood up with difficulty and followed the Labrador, his head low. The cat finished washing himself and danced into the sunlight. He played with a leaf and then ran straight to the dogs.

All that afternoon they walked along the quiet country road. When the young dog heard a car, they moved to the side, onto the grass. By late afternoon the cat was still walking smoothly and strongly, and the young dog was fresh too. But the old terrier was exhausted and could only walk very slowly. They turned off the road into the woods and the terrier stood for a minute, his heavy head down. He was tired and hungry, and the place looked safe and comfortable. He lay down on his side to rest his aching body. The cat looked around carefully and then lay down in the leaves near him. The young dog disappeared to find some water, then came back and lay down a little way from the others.

The old dog was shaking badly, exhausted and weak. At last his eyes closed and he fell asleep. Later, when it was dark, the Labrador moved over and lay down close to the bull terrier. The cat moved closer too and lay between his paws. And so, warm and comfortable with his two friends, the old dog forgot about the pain in his tired, aching body.

In the middle of the night a strange noise, like a baby's crying, woke the terrier up. When he looked around he couldn't see the cat. Tao was hunting in the woods.

The young dog slept badly. He often woke up, nervously lifting his head. He barked softly from time to time, and once jumped up to his feet. In this wild, dangerous place only one thing was clear to him: he was going home, home to his dear master. Home was in the west, he knew. But he couldn't leave the other two. He must take them with him, all the way.

Chapter 3   Danger! Bears!

In the early morning the bull terrier woke up and struggled to his feet. He was very cold, hungry, and thirsty. He walked slowly toward a pool, passing the cat with a bird in his paws on the way. The old dog watched the cat as he started to eat. His tail wagged with interest. The cat finished the bird, looked at Bodger, and then proudly walked away. There was no meat on the dead bird's body for the poor old terrier. He drank long and deeply from the pool and ate some grass. But he was still very hungry.

Soon the young dog walked over. Bodger was glad to see Luath and slowly followed him toward the road. A few seconds later the cat joined them. He was looking happy after his delicious breakfast.

In the gray light of early morning, the three friends continued along the side of the road. In the middle of the day they rested by a stream. The dogs watched the cat as he caught and killed a small animal. The terrier moved toward the cat with his mouth open and a hopeful look in his eyes. But Tao ran off with the animal and both dogs stayed hungry.

A few minutes later, the cat came back, sat down, and started washing himself. The old dog walked away to search for food. He found nothing. Sadly he lay down under a tree, put his paws on his dirty face, and washed himself. The Labrador wanted food too, but he wasn't a real hunter. He often went hunting with men, but not alone. He drank deeply at a stream and then they all started their journey again. The road went high over the hilly, wooded country. Below them, the land was full of incredibly beautiful colors: red, yellow, gold, and dark green.

Late in the afternoon the old dog slowed down. He was very weak and his body was shaking. The cat noticed this and started to walk closer to his struggling old friend. Finally the terrier stopped. He fell to the ground, closed his eyes, and didn't move. The young dog looked worried. He pushed the old dog with his nose again and again and barked loudly. The cat joined him and tried to wake the terrier up too. But Bodger didn't move.

The Labrador and the cat sat by the terrier's side, worried and afraid. At last they got up and left him. The Labrador disappeared into the trees and the cat started hunting for his supper.

It began to get dark and windy, but still the old dog didn't move. Leaves flew over him and covered his dirty, old body. Then the wind stopped and the wood was silent again.

Suddenly, there was a sound of a large animal in the wood. Out of the trees came a young, half-grown bear! Its round ears stood up and its small, curious eyes shone in its sharp little face. Its mother stood behind it, interested in something on the ground. The young bear saw the terrier and watched him for a minute. Then it slowly moved toward him.

The terrier opened his eyes. He could feel the danger near him. Then the bear put its long paw on the dog's white head. The terrier barked weakly and the bear jumped back. But the dog was quiet, so it came nearer again. The excited bear hit the terrier with its paw, harder this time. The old dog wasn't strong enough to fight back. He barked in pain, and bravely tried to struggle to his feet. The bear attacked his aching shoulder. The smell of blood excited it and it climbed on top of the dog's body. It started to play with the terrier's long white tail, biting the end of it like a child with a new toy. But the poor old dog couldn't move. He lay down with his eyes closed, feeling no pain.

Around the corner of the road came the cat with a large dead bird in his mouth. When he saw the bear, he stopped suddenly. He dropped the bird, and a terrible change took place in him. His huge blue eyes shone angrily in his dark face. Every hair on his body stood up, so he looked twice his real size. His chocolate-colored tail moved from side to side. He lay low on the ground, ready to attack. And when the bear turned around, the cat jumped.

The bear screamed in pain and fear as the cat landed on the

14

The bear screamed in pain and fear as the cat landed on the back of its neck.

back of its neck. Again and again the cat attacked, and the young bear's body was soon covered in blood. Its screams were answered by its mother. The great black bear hurried through the trees to protect her baby. She attacked the cat with a huge paw, but the cat was too quick for her. With a terrible, angry cry he jumped down to the ground and disappeared behind a tree.

The mother turned and saw the old dog. As she listened to the cries of fear and pain from the young bear, she felt crazy and angry. She stood up to her full height, ready for attack. Her red eyes shone angrily, and her head moved from side to side. The cat saw this. He ran back to help his friend.

When the mother bear heard the cat's terrible screams, she felt nervous and afraid. She lowered her head, and started to move back. Slowly, purposefully, the cat moved closer, and again the bear moved back. The cat stopped and moved his tail from side to side. The bear stopped too, afraid of this strange, terrible animal.

Suddenly, the Labrador jumped out from behind the trees, barking loudly. Every hair on his red–gold back stood up. When the bear saw the two of them, she ran toward her baby. There was one more cry from the bears and then they disappeared into the wood. Everything was quiet again.

The cat changed back to his usual size. His eyes became calm again and lost their angry look. He shook each paw and slowly walked back to his dead bird.

The young dog went over to his old friend and touched him lovingly with his nose. The terrier's body was covered in blood. The Labrador tried to clean it with his rough tongue. He barked near the old dog's head, but the terrier didn't move. At last the Labrador lay down next to him on the grass. His eyes were nervous, the hairs on his back stood up, and from time to time he barked. He watched Tao as he pulled a large gray bird up to the old dog's nose. Slowly the cat began to break open the bird's body, and soon the smell of the warm meat reached the terrier.

He opened one eye and wagged his tail. Then he sat up. He was shaking badly, and his body was wet and bloody. But when he saw the bird, he looked interested. He pushed his nose against it and began to eat. The cat sat down near him, proudly washing his tail.

The old dog ate quickly. As his friends watched, they could see his body get stronger. Then he slept, and by night he was able to walk to the soft grass at the side of the road with the Labrador. He lay down again. An hour or two later, the cat joined them, carelessly dropping another bird near his old friend's nose. The terrier ate it quickly and then went to sleep.

The cat sat against his chest and the young dog lay at his back. They stayed awake, looking for signs of danger. Neither animal moved from their old friend's side all night.

Chapter 4   The White Dog of the Indians

The next day the old terrier was still weak and exhausted after the adventure with the bear. There was blood all over his aching body. All day he lay on the grass in the warm fall sunshine, sleeping deeply. He wagged his tail when one of his friends came near.

The Labrador was now very hungry, but he wasn't a skillful hunter. He spent the day searching for food. In the evening, at last, he succeeded in catching a small animal. He ate the delicious, warm meat quickly.

They slept in the same place that night and most of the following day. The weather continued warm and sunny. By the third day the old dog seemed better and was able to walk around comfortably. So, in the late afternoon, they started their journey again.

They walked slowly along the road for a few kilometers and arrived at a small lake. They were sitting at the side of the lake when the young dog suddenly turned his head. He could smell wood smoke far away...Seconds later, the old dog smelled it too and got up. His thin tail began to wag from side to side and his black eyes shone in his old white face. Somewhere, not too far away, were human beings. His world! He couldn't refuse their invitation: they were cooking something delicious. He hurried off toward the wonderful smell. The young dog followed more slowly and the cat ran past them both.

The smell was coming from wood smoke, rice, and chicken. When the hungry animals looked down from the hill, they saw some small boats by the side of a lake. Near the boats were six or seven fires, and tents in the trees. In the light of the fires they could see the flat, brown faces of North American Indians, talking in the firelight.

The men looked colorful in jeans and bright shirts, but the women were dressed in dark colors. Two young boys, the only children there, were moving from fire to fire. They were helping to cook the rice and meat. Some of the men lay back from the fires, smoking lazily. They talked quietly to each other.

The old dog couldn't see all this clearly. But he could hear and smell everything and couldn't wait. He walked carefully down the hill because his shoulder was still aching. One of the boys looked up and watched the terrier. Bodger came out of the shadows and into the firelight, friendly and sure of a warm welcome. His tail wagged from side to side and he had his big, ugly smile on his face.

There was a surprised silence and then the smaller boy started to cry. He ran to his mother and the Indians all started talking excitedly. For a second the old dog didn't know what to do. Then he walked toward the nearest boy, hopefully. The boy ran away, but his mother came toward the old dog. She spoke some soft words to him, touched his head, and smiled at him. The old dog wagged his tail against her legs, happy to be near a human being again. The

18

two boys moved closer. The other Indians came nearer too. This was what the old dog loved. There were people all around him. They gave him meat and he ate it hungrily. They laughed and gave him more. Soon he grew tired and lay down, warm and happy. Then he looked up at the hillside for his two friends.

Next the long-legged, blue-eyed cat came out of the darkness. He walked up to the dog and calmly took a piece of meat from him. The Indians couldn't stop laughing. The two little boys lay on the ground, kicking their legs with excitement. The terrier loved children and started playing with them.

All this time the young dog stayed on the hillside, watching his friends below with the Indians. He saw the cat, well fed and happy, lying by the fire in the arms of one of the sleepy children. He saw one of the Indian women washing the blood from the terrier's body. Then she put a piece of meat on the grass in front of the old dog. The hungry Labrador watched as the terrier ate it.

When the fires began to burn low, the Indians got ready for bed. But the old dog and the cat were comfortable and didn't move. The young dog on the hillside started barking. When they heard him, the other two woke up. The cat jumped down from the arms of the sleepy little Indian boy and ran toward the terrier. He shook himself and walked slowly after the cat, away from the warm fire. The Indians watched silently. They didn't try to stop the animals. Only the mother called out softly, saying goodbye to the travelers.

The old dog looked back once or twice, but he could hear the Labrador's loud bark. Then the two animals disappeared into the blackness of the night.

The Indians never forgot their two visitors. The old dog became the famous "White Dog of the Indians." "He was sent to bring us luck," they said. "We welcomed him, fed him, and looked after him. We will have great luck in the future."

Chapter 5   An Invitation to Dinner

The three friends continued on their journey for the next few days with no new adventures or excitement. At night they slept in the woods, warm and comfortable under the leaves on the ground. At first, in the day, they often stopped and rested. The old dog was too weak to go far. But he got stronger every day and after a week looked much better. In fact, he looked younger and healthier than at the beginning of the journey. Most of the time he was happy as he walked along with his friends. He was always hungry, but the skillful hunter, the cat, found food for him.

But the Labrador really suffered. He had very little to eat. While the other two animals were resting, he always looked for food. When they played together, he sat away from them, nervous and uncomfortable. He could never forget his purpose: he was going home. He belonged at home with his master. Nothing mattered except this. And he had to take his two friends with him, through wild, unknown country.

They traveled along old country roads and sometimes straight through fields and woods. On good days they walked as many as twenty-five kilometers. The weather was fine, with warm, sunny days. This was a good thing because the bull terrier's hair was short and thin. The Labrador's hair was flat and thick and he never felt the cold like the old dog. The cat was enjoying the adventure, sometimes leaving the other two for an hour or more. They didn't worry, as he always returned.

The days were warm but the nights were cold, and the old dog suffered then. The leaves on the trees were quickly losing their color. Many of the birds of the forest started to fly to warmer places in the south.

Once they saw another bear, but it was fat and sleepy. It was sitting in the sun when the three friends saw it. It looked up lazily but wasn't interested in them. But the cat looked angry for about an hour after this meeting. The animals didn't see any more human beings for days.

Then one day, when the old dog was alone, he saw an old man. The terrier loved people and his tail began to wag from side to side in welcome. The man was carrying a bag and talking quietly to himself. When he saw the old dog, he lifted his old green hat from his white hair. He smiled kindly at the terrier and said hello. The old dog started to follow him. Soon the cat followed too, and far behind them came the Labrador.

After about a kilometer, they arrived at a small cabin and walked through the yard to the front steps. Here the old man put his bag down and opened the green door. He then invited his new friends to come in. The old dog walked in with the cat near his shoulder, then the man. The young dog waited outside, unsure at first, and then followed the others. A delicious, meaty smell filled the front room.

The old man hung up his hat, walked over to the fire, and put on some more wood. He washed his hands and then looked in a pot on the stove. The three hungry animals watched him carefully. The man took four plates from a cupboard and put them on the table. As he put the food on the plates, the old dog moved nearer.

The old man sat down, looked around the table, and said, "Please, sit down."

The three animals sat down on the floor behind him and waited patiently.

The old man ate slowly and carefully as the animals watched. Soon his plate was empty. Then he looked around the table and said, in a surprised voice, "You haven't eaten your food!" He looked at the three full plates thoughtfully for a long time. Then he got up, picked up one of them, and ate all the food on it. He got up again and picked up the second plate. When that was empty, he ate the food on the third plate. His three visitors sat and watched. None of them moved. They never jumped up on chairs

21

They arrived at a small cabin.

and ate at the table with the Hunters or with Longridge. So they stayed politely on the floor and waited. But they felt very, very hungry.

The old man sat at the table when the last plate was empty. He was lost in his private thoughts and forgot about his visitors. After some time a bird flew in through the window and broke the silence. The old man got up, looked around, and noticed the animals by the door. He looked surprised and smiled down at them kindly.

"You must come more often," he said. Then he looked at the old dog. He was wagging his tail. "Please say hello to your dear mother from me!"

He opened the door for the animals. They walked out, through the yard, and into the wood, their heads down and their tails low. None of them looked back at the old man.

Chapter 6   Lost in the River

The next day the travelers came down from the hills to a river which ran from north to south. It was very wide and deep. The Labrador knew that his two friends hated water. They didn't even like getting their feet wet. But they all had to get across to the other side.

Luath tried to find a shallow part of the river. Once or twice he went into the water and swam around. He looked back at the other two, inviting them in. But they stayed on the side of the river, sitting close together.

In this lonely, wild country there were no human beings and no bridges. The young dog continued searching for an easy place to cross. But the river got wider and wider, and after four or five kilometers he lost patience. He ran into the water and swam quickly and strongly to the other side. He loved the water and felt completely comfortable in it. He stood on the other side of the river, looking back at the old dog and the cat. He barked loudly, but they looked nervous and afraid.

At last, the young dog swam back to his friends and waited in the shallow water. The terrier joined him, but he was shaking with cold and fear. Once again the Labrador swam across the river, climbed out onto the far side, shook himself, and barked. His bark meant: "You two must follow me! Come on! It's easy!"

The old dog stepped into the water. The Labrador swam back to help him. This happened three times, and the third time the old dog walked into the river up to his chest. Then he started swimming. He wasn't a very good swimmer: he held his head high out of the water, and his little black eyes looked scared. But he was a brave bull terrier and he continued following the Labrador. At last he reached the other side and climbed out onto dry land. He ran around happily, lay on his back, and dried himself in the long grass. Then he joined the Labrador at the side of the river and barked at the cat.

The poor cat now showed the first signs of fear on the journey. He was alone and didn't want to swim across this terrible river. But he had to join his friends on the other side. He ran up and down, crying out to the other two animals. The young dog swam back and waited in the water.

After a long time, the cat suddenly decided to cross. He ran into the water and started swimming toward the Labrador. He was a surprisingly good swimmer, quickly reaching the middle of the river. But then a terrible accident happened!

There was an old dam on a smaller stream that ran into the river about three kilometers away. It was built from small trees and pieces of wood and wasn't very strong. Suddenly it broke, and a wave of water poured into the river and hit the two animals! The brave young dog tried to protect the cat, but he was too late. The wave passed over them and a large piece of wood hit the cat on the head. He was swept under and over and over, and was carried away down the river.

The old dog barked wildly on the side of the river. Then he jumped into the water and swam. He tried to save the cat but the water knocked him back and he had to swim to the side again. The young dog was a strong swimmer but he swam with great difficulty. The river carried him a kilometer before he could put his feet down. When he reached dry land, he quickly climbed out onto the grass. He ran down the side of the river, looking for the cat. He could see his little body, half under water. But he was never near enough to catch his friend.

Soon Luath was far behind and couldn't see Tao at all. He came to a place where steep rocks formed the side of the river. The path took him high above the water. When it came down again, there was no sign of the cat.

It was almost dark when the Labrador returned to the terrier. Bodger was walking toward him along the river, tired and unhappy. The Labrador was exhausted too. He greeted the old dog and then dropped to the ground. He only got up when he needed a drink.

They spent that night by the side of the river. They lay close together to get comfortable and warm. When a thin, cold rain fell, they moved under an old tree.

In the middle of the night the old dog sat up, shaking with cold. He threw his head back and cried out to the heavy, black sky. He missed his dear, lost friend. He wanted to see him by his side again. At last the young dog got up sadly and the two started their lonely journey again, away from the river and over the hills to the west.

Chapter 7   A Loving Family

Many kilometers down the river there was a small cabin, with beautiful red flowers in the windows, and a blue front door. Vegetables grew in the yard, and there were apple trees and green fields around the house.

Reino Nurmi and his wife lived here. They came from Finland and had a ten-year-old daughter, Helvi. Life was hard in this wild place near the forest. But the Nurmis were strong people. They worked hard and had a good, simple life. They ate the food that they grew. They caught fish in the river and sold wood.

Unlike her parents, Helvi was born in Canada. Every day she walked through the lonely country to the school bus. And every afternoon, when she came home, she told her parents about life outside their small farm.

One Sunday afternoon, Helvi was playing down by the river. She was throwing stones across the water. She was lonely and wanted a friend to play with. Suddenly, a big wave came past. Helvi was safe because she wasn't standing in the river. She stood and watched, then saw something strange. What was it? It looked like a small, wet body! It turned round and round in the water, and was then pushed onto the rocks.

Helvi ran along by the water to look more closely. Then she shouted out to her mother.

"Mother! Mother! Come here quickly! There's a strange animal in the river! It's caught in the rocks!"

Mrs. Nurmi was out in the yard, planting vegetables. She hurried down to the side of the river, calling to her husband at the same time.

He followed her, walking calmly with a quiet, thoughtful face. They all looked down in silence at the small, thin body on the rocks. Then Mr. Nurmi put his hand lightly on it and pulled back the skin above and below one eye.

26

He turned and saw Helvi's worried face close to his. "This cat's been in the water for a long time," he said. "He's very weak. Shall we try to save him?"

Helvi and her mother both wanted to save the poor animal. So Mr. Nurmi picked up the wet cat and walked back to the cabin.

He put the cat down in a sunny place by the fire and dried him. Then Helvi's mother opened his teeth and Helvi poured a little warm milk into his mouth. The cat shook, coughed, and some milk came out of his mouth. Mr. Nurmi pressed his body. The cat coughed again and a stream of river water came out of his mouth. Then he lay down and went to sleep.

Mr. Nurmi smiled happily. "Keep him warm and quiet," he told Helvi. "But are you sure you want a cat?"

"Oh yes!" answered Helvi, as she looked down at the sleeping animal by the fire.

Her mother went into the kitchen to make supper. Her father left to feed the chickens. Helvi sat by the cat and watched patiently. Sometimes she put her hand near the fire and touched the soft, warm body. After about half an hour the cat woke up. Helvi looked closely into the bright blue eyes. The cat looked back and slowly started to move. Very excited, Helvi called to her parents.

After another half hour, she was holding the Siamese cat in her arms. Then she gave him some milk. He usually hated milk, but he drank it quickly. Then he started washing himself from head to foot. As the Nurmi family ate their supper, he finished a bowl of meat. Then he walked around the table legs, asking for more food, his tail straight in the air. Helvi thought he was wonderful.

That night the Nurmis were having fresh fish. It was cooked in the country way with the head still on, in a soup with potatoes. Helvi put the head with some soup and potatoes into a bowl and placed it on the floor. The cat ate everything, holding the bowl down with his paws. Happy at last, he lay down near Helvi's feet

27

and went to sleep. For the first time in her life, Helvi had her own pet.

Helvi carried the cat up to bed with her. He lay on her shoulder as she climbed the steep stairs to her little room at the top of the house. She put him into the old wooden bed that she slept in as a baby. He went to sleep there happily.

Late in the night she woke up when the cat climbed on her back. The weather outside was cold, wet, and windy. Helvi got up to shut the window. Then she lay down again and felt the warm, comfortable body of the cat on her bed.

When Helvi left in the morning for the long walk and ride to school, the cat lay by the window. His hair shone in the sun as he washed himself sleepily. His eyes followed Mrs. Nurmi as she moved about the cabin. She went outside with the washing and looked back at the cat. He was standing on his back legs, looking out at her. His mouth was opening and shutting behind the window. She ran back, opened the door, and he followed her to the washing line. He sat by her and then followed her around the cabin and yard all morning. When she shut him in the cabin once by mistake, he cried out loudly.

He followed the Nurmis around all day.

"Why is he watching us all the time?" Mrs. Nurmi asked her husband. "Maybe he needs to be near people."

But her husband noticed the worried look in the cat's blue eyes. When a bird flew near him, he didn't look up.

"No, it's because he can't hear," Mr. Nurmi said. "I think the poor cat's deaf!"

Helvi ran most of the way home across the fields. When she saw the cat, she picked him up. He sat on her shoulder while she helped her mother with the supper. She saw that her father was right. The cat was deaf and his ears didn't turn toward any sound.

After supper her parents sat by the fire and Helvi read to them.

For the first time in her life, Helvi had her own pet.

Because they were Finnish, they couldn't read English. But Helvi learned English every day at school, so she helped them with the new language. They sat and rested, with the cat near their feet, and listened to the child's soft voice. She had a book about Siamese cats: great, proud Siamese cats from all over the world. As they listened, they looked down at their visitor. He lay in front of the fire with his tail sometimes moving. His beautiful blue eyes watched their daughter's hand as she turned the pages of the book. They touched his soft body and wonderful tail. Then Helvi gave him a bowl of milk. He drank it proudly, like a king, before she carried him upstairs to bed.

That night, and for one more night, the cat lay happily in Helvi's arms. In the daytime, while she was at school, he followed her parents everywhere. He walked close to her mother as she looked for wood in the forest. He sat at her feet on the front steps as she prepared vegetables in the sun. He followed Mr. Nurmi and his work horse across the fields. And in the late afternoons, when Helvi came back from school, he was waiting for her. He was one of the family.

But on the fourth night he changed. He didn't seem comfortable on Helvi's bed. He shook his head and cried out unhappily. At last he lay down and pushed his head into her hand. She noticed that his ears were moving; he could hear every sound in the night outside! She was happy that he wasn't deaf any more. Soon she fell asleep.

When she woke up later in the night, the bed felt cold. She saw the cat near the open window, looking out over the pale fields at the tall, dark trees below. His long tail moved from side to side. She put out her hand, but he suddenly jumped out of the window onto the soft ground below.

She looked down and called out. His head turned for the first time to her voice. His eyes shone in the moonlight and then he turned away. She realized sadly that he was leaving. He didn't need her now. Crying, she watched him go into the night. He walked toward the river. Soon the running shadow of the cat was lost in the other shadows.

Chapter 8   A Cat Fight

The cat was a fast traveler. Only the rain slowed him down. He hated the wet and hid under a tree with his ears back. When the rain stopped completely, he came out. He walked uncomfortably through the wet grass and often shook his paws.

Without his noisier friends, the dogs, the curious cat saw everything. He watched the forest animals, but they couldn't see him. When he met an animal face to face, it turned away. He only slept a little, up in the trees. He was a smart and skillful traveler, afraid of nothing.

Early on the second morning of his travels alone, he went down to a lake to drink. He suddenly saw two men on the side of the lake with guns across their knees, and a dog. The men called out to him, but the cat didn't look up. He put his pink tongue in the water and drank slowly. Both men called out again, amused by the cat. At last he looked up, shook each paw, and calmly walked away. Behind him the men started laughing as the proud cat continued his journey.

♦

The two dogs felt very sad as they traveled without the cat. Tao was the terrier's oldest friend and he missed him a lot. The Labrador loved the cat too, but Tao and Bodger were special friends. The two dogs tried to hunt for food, but without the cat's help they didn't do very well.

One day they walked near a farm. The young dog didn't want to meet any human beings, but he was hungry. They crossed an open field to steal one of the farmer's chickens. Suddenly, they heard an angry shout and saw a man at the far corner of the field. A black farm dog was with him. It ran to attack them.

The Labrador was a terrible fighter and was hungry and weak. He was on his back, with the farm dog on top of him, when brave Bodger jumped at the farm dog's neck. He knocked him over. The farm dog struggled to his feet and the terrier knocked him over again. Then he turned and proudly walked away. The farm dog, usually very brave, stood up shakily. His neck was covered in blood. He ran away toward his master. The farmer watched the two dogs running away across the field with one of his chickens.

"Come back here!" he shouted angrily, but the dogs were too far away.

Bodger felt stronger and braver after this fight. That evening he caught a small animal and had a delicious supper. Luath was badly hurt, but he seemed happier too. Maybe it was because he could feel the west wind. Memories of home came back to him. He knew that every day, every hour, they were getting nearer.

◆

The cat was following the Labrador and the old terrier. He knew which way to go. He could smell his friends clearly. But he began to feel nervous and afraid. Something was wrong, something bad was following him. He started to walk through the forest more quickly, looking for the blue sky and open country far in front of him.

Suddenly, every hair on his back stood up! He could hear and feel an animal behind him. And it was not far away! The cat jumped up into a tree and looked down. There, moving silently through the forest, was a huge cat! And it was very different from an ordinary cat like Tao.

This one was almost twice as large, heavy, with a short tail and thick legs. Its coat was soft gray, and darker in some places. It had

There, moving silently through the forest, was a huge cat!

the wild face of a killer, much stronger and faster than Tao. It was a lynx! Tao quickly climbed to the top of the tree. The lynx heard him and stopped suddenly. It looked up, lifting one heavy paw. Its terrible eyes shone angrily. The cat looked around nervously, searching for a way to escape. His tail moved from side to side and he made a low, scared noise.

Then the lynx started climbing the tree toward the cat. As its heavy body came nearer, the tree moved dangerously. The cat found it difficult to hold on. Then the lynx attacked with its great paw. The cat hit back, the tree moved wildly, and the cat fell to the ground. He heard the lynx land near him, got up fast, and ran for his life.

Almost immediately he heard the lynx close behind him. The cat couldn't turn and fight: this was a dangerous enemy, not a stupid bear. As he ran away, he knew it was hopeless. Every time the cat climbed up a tree, the lynx followed. Its great size shook the tree, and the cat fell off again and again. Then he saw a hole in the ground and ran into it. The hole was too small for the lynx to follow. It lay on the ground and looked into the hole with one terrible green eye. But it soon moved back when some earth hit it in the face. The cat's back legs were working hard, throwing earth out of the hole!

The lynx sat back and thought. There was complete silence in the forest. Deep in the hole, the cat waited, too scared to do anything. Suddenly, the lynx began to push the earth around the hole to one side with its huge paws. It didn't hear a young boy behind it. The boy was wearing a bright red jacket and carrying a gun. He was hunting, so he walked softly. Suddenly, he saw the wild animal at the entrance to the hole. At exactly the same time, the lynx saw the boy. It made a terrible noise. No fear showed in its angry eyes as it moved toward the boy. In a second, the boy lifted his gun and shot, all in one quick movement. The lynx turned over in the air and fell. It hit the ground and lay there, dead.

The boy was shaking as he moved toward the dead animal. He couldn't forget the crazy look in the lynx's eyes. He looked down at it with a pale face but he couldn't touch it. The boy's father hurried toward his son. He stopped suddenly when he saw the huge body on the ground and his son's white face.

The man turned the animal over. "Look, son," he said to the boy, smiling. "Look at that hole. That's where you shot it!"

The boy smiled back, still shaking.

"Tie this red cloth on the tree, son," said his father. "Then it'll be easy to find. We'll come back later."

The boy tied the cloth tightly on the tree and looked down at the lynx one more time. Then father and son walked away together, talking excitedly. The hidden cat could hear their voices for a long time.

When everything was silent, he came out of his hiding place into the sun. He was tired and dirty. He didn't look at the dead body once. He calmly walked around it, sat down near it, and started washing his body from the end of his tail to his nose. Then he continued on his way, as calm and proud as always.

◆

Two days later, the cat found the two dogs. He came down a hill into a valley and suddenly saw his dear golden and white friends on the other side of a small stream. His tail moved in excitement, he opened his mouth and cried out. The two dogs stopped immediately, listening to the unbelievable sound in the valley. The cat jumped up onto a rock so that they could see him clearly. The young dog started to bark loudly and hurried across the stream. The old dog followed and the cat began to run too. They met near the little stream, all of them very excited.

In his happiness, the old dog knocked the cat over twice with his head! The cat ran straight up a tree and then dropped down onto the old dog's back! The young dog stood there, slowly wagging his tail. When the old dog was too tired to move, the Labrador walked up to the cat. Tao stood on his back legs and put his chocolate-colored front paws on the great dog's neck.

That night the three friends were happier than any other animals in the world. They lay close together under an old tree near the stream. Bodger had his dear cat, warm and loving, between his paws again. Luath stopped worrying. His friend was back and he could continue the journey with a lighter heart.

Chapter 9 A Welcome Rest

Longridge's house was now three hundred kilometers behind them. The three animals were all alive, but only the cat was really healthy. The old dog still struggled along happily, but the Labrador was really weak after the fight with the farm dog. His beautiful red-gold coat didn't shine. He couldn't open his mouth fully because of an aching tooth, so he was hungry all the time. When the cat killed a small animal or bird, he gave it to the Labrador. But the young dog could only drink the fresh blood of the animal.

Every day the two dogs walked along side by side, brave and purposeful. They looked like two family pets out for a walk around the neighborhood. One morning they were seen like this by a man who was working in the forest. He was busy with the trees and didn't think about them at the time. But later in the day, when he remembered the two dogs, he was surprised. There were no houses for forty kilometers. So where did the dogs come from? He told his boss but his boss just laughed. He thought that his friend was imagining things!

"What will you start dreaming about next?" he asked.

But a few days later, people started to talk about the disappearance of the three animals. And then the boss stopped laughing.

♦

At Heron Lake, the vacation of John Longridge and his brother was ending. In England, the excited Hunter family were packed and ready to return home. Mrs. Oakes was busy in the old stone house, while her husband worked in the yard.

At the same time, the three animals continued on their way. The country was less wild now, and once or twice they saw small, lonely houses. The young dog stayed in the woods and didn't go near them. But the old dog loved human beings and looked at the houses with hopeful eyes.

Late one afternoon they were followed by a bear. It was curious about the animals but was no danger to them. The young dog felt uncomfortable, though, with the shadow of the great bear behind them. He decided to leave the woods and walk along a quiet country road. As it got dark, they arrived at a few small houses, a schoolhouse, and a white church. The young dog wanted to continue, but the old dog suddenly refused to move. He was, as usual, very hungry. And when he saw the warm lights from the houses, he wanted food, from the hand of a human being. His eyes grew bright at the thought and he started to walk toward the houses. The young dog followed. He felt weak and sick after the fight with the farm dog. His bad tooth was very painful. He wanted to lie down and rest his aching head on the ground.

As they passed the first houses, they could smell the delicious smell of supper. They heard the sounds of human beings everywhere. The old dog stopped outside one of the houses. He walked up the steps, lifted his paw, and knocked on the door. Then he sat down and listened hopefully.

Soon the door opened and a small girl stood in front of him. The old dog looked up at her with his ugly smile on his face. The girl looked afraid and shouted out, "Dad!…" Then the door shut hard in the terrier's face.

The old dog couldn't understand, but knocked again. He saw a face at the window and barked politely at it. Suddenly, the door was thrown open again and a man ran out with a bowl of water in his hand. Angry, he threw the water in the old dog's face. "Get out! Get out of here!" the man shouted. The wet terrier ran away fast toward the Labrador and the cat. He wasn't afraid but he felt unhappy. Human beings were not usually like that when he was friendly to them. They always laughed and played with him.

He quietly followed the Labrador back along the road. Three kilometers later, they arrived at a farm. They crossed some dark fields and lay down for the night outside one of the farm buildings.

The young dog had a bad night. His mouth was aching and he was exhausted with the pain. He got up in the night to drink from a small lake. He stood chest-deep in the cold water.

When the old dog woke up in the morning, he was alone. The cat was hunting for his breakfast and the young dog was down by the lake. The terrier could smell cooking through the morning air. The pale sun was coming up in the sky as he walked to the farmhouse door. He sat down on the steps and waited. His memory was short; human beings were friendly again and gave dogs food. He knocked on the door with his paw. It opened and a wonderful smell of breakfast came out. The terrier smiled his ugly smile. There was a silence, then the deep, amused voice of a man said, "Who's here?" He looked down at his strange visitor, then called into the house. "Come here a minute, dear, and look at this!"

The warm voice of a woman answered, and then she stood next to the man at the open door. She looked down in surprise at the white dog on the step. When he saw her smile, the old terrier gave her his paw. She shook it, laughing quietly. Then she invited him into the house.

The old dog walked in calmly and looked around for food. He

"Come here a minute, dear, and look at this!"

was lucky because this man and woman were the kindest people in the neighborhood. Their house was the most welcoming. James and Nell Mackenzie lived alone in the big farmhouse. Their eight children were adults now and lived away from home.

Nell gave their visitor a bowl of food and he ate it quickly. Then he looked up for more. "He's very hungry!" she said, and gave him her breakfast. He ate that almost before it reached the ground. Without a word James Mackenzie gave him his plate of food too. And some milk. At last, warm and happy, the old dog lay down in front of the fire while Nell cooked another breakfast.

"What type of dog is he?" she asked. "I've never seen anything so friendly. But he's ugly too!"

"He's an English bull terrier," said her husband. "I love them. He's about ten or eleven years old. And I think he's been in a fight."

The old dog listened and wagged his tail from side to side. Then he got up and put his head on Mackenzie's knee. "You *are* friendly, aren't you? But what are we going to do with you?"

Nell touched the dog's shoulder and then looked at him more closely. "He hasn't been in a dog fight," she said. "He's had a fight with a bear!"

In silence they looked down at the dog by their feet. They could see now that he was exhausted. He had a look of sadness in his little eyes and he was too thin. This wasn't a brave adventurer— only a tired old dog, hungry for food and love.

"We'll keep him if he wants to stay," Nell said.

"I'll tell the police when I go into Deepwater," said Mackenzie. "Maybe we can write something about the dog for the city newspaper too. If nobody wants him, he can live with us."

After breakfast Mackenzie went down to a small lake to do some hunting. Six birds flew into the air and he shot at them twice. One bird fell into the water and another on the ground near the lake. He picked one up and then, to his surprise, saw the large head of a dog in the lake! It was swimming toward the dead bird! The Labrador caught the bird, swam out of the water with it, and brought it to the man.

Mackenzie couldn't believe it. "Good dog!" he said quietly, holding out one hand. "Well done! Now give it to me."

The dog walked slowly toward the man and put down the bird. Mackenzie saw that he was in great pain and needed help. He picked up the bird and said, "Follow me," to the Labrador.

The dog walked behind him back to the farmhouse. He was too weak to worry about human beings.

Crossing the fields with the dog at his side, Mackenzie thought about the other dog. How many more were there in the neighborhood? "Maybe another one will come to the kitchen door this afternoon!" he laughed to himself.

As Mackenzie passed one of the farm buildings, a sleepy Siamese cat looked up. The farmer didn't see him, but the young dog wagged his tail and turned his head.

In the kitchen, the man looked in the Labrador's mouth and carefully cleaned his bad tooth. Then he gave him some medicine to help the pain. While Mackenzie was helping Luath, the terrier watched closely. He didn't want the man to hurt his dear friend.

After about an hour, the Labrador looked much better. The old dog sat next to him as he drank a bowl of milk. It was clear to the Mackenzies that the two dogs came from the same home. But they couldn't understand why the animals weren't with their family.

"What are they doing out in this wild country?" Nell asked.

"Maybe their master's died," Mackenzie answered, "and they've run away together. Or maybe they were in a car with someone but got lost. You can see that they've been away from home a long time. And they've been very hungry. How did they find enough food to stay alive?"

"Hunting? Stealing maybe?" Nell suggested. "I saw the old dog take some food off a plate on the table after breakfast!"

"So they didn't eat much in the forest," said her husband thoughtfully. "The Labrador's very thin. I'll shut them in one of the farm buildings outside when I go to Deepwater, Nell. We don't want them to run away. Now, are you sure you want these two strange dogs?"

"I want them," she said, "if they'll stay. But we must think of names for them. We can't say 'good dog' all the time. I'll think of some names while you're in Deepwater."

Mackenzie crossed the yard with the two dogs and put them in one of the warm, sweet-smelling farm buildings. Then he shut the door carefully behind him. The cat sat in the sun and watched. Soon Mackenzie drove away and everything was quiet again. A few curious farm cats came to look at Tao. Who was this stranger in their favorite place in the sun? Tao didn't like other cats and watched them coldly. After two or three small fights, the farm cats walked away and Tao went back to sleep.

Halfway through the morning, he woke up and walked toward the farm building. He skillfully opened the door with his paws and walked in. His old friends welcomed him loudly and followed him into the sunny yard.

When Mackenzie drove into the yard later in the afternoon, he was surprised to see the two dogs outside in the sun. They stood up when they saw him. Then, with wagging tails, they followed him into the house.

"Did you let them out into the yard, Nell?" he asked.

"Of course not," she answered in surprise. "I took them some milk, but I shut the door carefully after me."

"That's strange. We're lucky they're still here," said Mackenzie. "The Labrador looks much better. He'll be able to eat a good meal this evening. I'd like to see him fatter. Nobody knew about the dogs in Deepwater. But they came from the east because somebody in a town to the east saw them on his doorstep. Maybe the Labrador was on a hunting trip and got lost. But what about the bull terrier? Why is he with the young dog? If we don't want the dogs, somebody in Deepwater will take them."

"No they won't!" Nell said.

"All right," her husband agreed, laughing. "We'll keep them as long as we can, dear. But if they're going somewhere with a purpose, Nell, nothing will keep them here. We can feed them well. Then, if they leave, they'll have a better start."

After supper that night the Mackenzies and their guests moved into the little back room. It was warm and comfortable, with children's books, pictures, and photos of the family. Mackenzie sat at the table, smoking his pipe. His wife read a book. The Labrador lay under the table in a deep sleep, warm and safe. The terrier slept near him on an old sofa.

The only sound during the evening was the noise of a huge cat fight out in the yard. Both dogs sat up immediately, wagging their tails. "They look very interested," said Nell to her husband.

Later, the dogs followed Mackenzie out to the farm building. He filled a bowl with water, then shut the door behind him. A few minutes later, the lights in the house went out.

The dogs lay quietly in the darkness, waiting. Soon they heard the soft sound of paws on wood, and the door opened. The cat walked in and lay down next to the old dog's chest. Then there was silence in the building.

The young dog woke up in the cold early morning. He knew that they had to start their journey to the west again. The cat joined him at the door. Then the old dog came, shaking in the cold wind. For a few minutes they sat there quietly, listening. They could hear some of the farm animals moving. They looked across the dark yard. Then they silently crossed it, went into the fields, and started to walk west.

In front of them lay the last eighty kilometers of their journey. This country was more dangerous and lonely than before. And the young dog was already sick and weak.

Chapter 10   The Search Begins

The Hunter family were on their way home from England. The children, Peter and Elizabeth, were very excited. They wanted to see their home and friends again and, of course, their wonderful pets. Every day Elizabeth said to her mother, "I hope Tao hasn't forgotten me." She had a special present from England for him.

Peter wasn't worried about seeing Bodger again. He knew that his old terrier couldn't forget him. Their father was excited too. He wanted to see Luath again and go hunting with him.

Far away in Ontario, John Longridge returned from his vacation to an empty house. He looked for the animals everywhere: in the house, in the yard, in the fields. He called and called, but there was no answer.

Mrs. Oakes didn't know where they were either. She showed Longridge the first page of his note to her and the burnt second page.

"I only read the first page," said Mrs. Oakes. "I thought the animals were with you at Heron Lake."

"No, the animals have disappeared," Longridge said sadly. "But they were happy here. Why did they leave?"

"And why didn't anybody see them?" asked Mrs. Oakes sadly.

"I don't know. I've spoken to some of Bodger's friends at the school. None of the children saw the dogs or the cat on the day I left for my vacation. And the police don't know anything either."

Longridge went to sit down at his desk. He read a letter from Elizabeth again. She was excited about seeing Tao, and the dogs. In twenty-four hours he must tell the Hunters the terrible news about their lost pets. And he had no idea where they were!

He pressed his aching head into his hands and tried to think clearly. Animals didn't just disappear. Then he remembered Luath on the last morning...his eyes...Something was different...lifting up his paw. Suddenly, he understood!

He pressed his aching head into his hands and tried to think clearly.

"Mrs. Oakes!" he shouted. "I know what's happened! I know where they've gone! Luath's taken them home! He's taken them all back to their home!"

Mrs. Oakes looked at him in silence for a minute. Then she cried out, "No! It's not possible! The Hunters live more than four hundred kilometers away! And nobody's seen them…"

"There aren't many people if you go straight across country, over the Ironmouth mountains," said Longridge thoughtfully.

"Over the Ironmouth?" Mrs. Oakes said. "If you're right, then there's no hope. There are bears and other wild animals over there, and no food…"

"Maybe a hunter or somebody has helped them," said Longridge when he saw Mrs. Oakes's sad face.

"No, Mr. Longridge, it's impossible. A young dog could cross that country, and possibly a cat. A cat can look after itself. But old Bodger couldn't walk ten kilometers! No dog as old as Bodger could live more than a day or two in that wild country. And that's a fact."

They both looked out of the window at the dark.

"You're right, Mrs. Oakes," said Longridge in an exhausted voice. "They left almost three weeks ago. I'm sure our old friend Bodger is dead. And Tao too, maybe. Siamese cats hate the cold. But a big, strong dog like Luath may still be alive."

"That Luath!" said Mrs. Oakes angrily. "Why did Bodger follow him to his death? And why didn't Tao stop Luath? Poor old Bodger."

She left the room quickly and shut the door. Longridge knew that she was crying about the animals.

With no time to lose, he phoned the police. "I'm sure the animals are trying to get home," he told him. "Can you ask everyone in the area to look for them?"

"Yes, of course, Mr. Longridge," the officer replied. "Everybody will help. But we can't do anything until tomorrow morning."

Longridge found a map of the area and drew a line between his small town and the Hunters' town. The line passed through hills, woods, and lakes, but not through many towns. The last seventy or eighty kilometers looked very wild and dangerous. Longridge felt less and less hopeful as he looked at the map. "Why did I offer to take the animals when the Hunters went to England?" he thought to himself. "Now they're dead, because of me. And tomorrow Elizabeth and Peter are coming home…"

Later that night the telephone rang. It was a hunter in a place called Lintola. "A little girl from the Nurmi family found a Siamese cat in the river about two weeks ago," he told Longridge. "But it disappeared again a few days later."

"Thank you," said Longridge. "I'll phone Lintola tomorrow and try to speak to the child."

"There's some other news too," the man said. "But I don't know if it's useful. Old Jeremy Aubyn came into town and talked about 'three visitors' to his house. He never has any visitors, poor old man. Maybe his visitors were animals, not people."

Longridge thanked the man warmly, put down the phone, and looked at Lintola on the map. "They *are* going home," he thought. "I was right. Two weeks ago the cat was alive. But what's happened to the other two? Are they dead?"

He lay awake in the dark that night, missing the feeling of the old terrier's warm body next to him on the bed.

"You can *have* the bed if you come back, Bodger," he thought. "I'll sleep on the floor. But please, come back!"

Chapter 11 Coming Home

In the following week Longridge's telephone never stopped ringing. Some of the news was difficult to believe. Some of it was hopeful. Longridge listened to it all patiently.

"Every man, woman, or child has seen a cat or dog on the road," said Longridge, exhausted, on the phone to Jim Hunter. "And they're all ringing to tell us!"

"Yes, but they're all trying to be helpful and kind," said Jim Hunter. "And some of them really *did* see our dear pets."

"We know from these phone calls that I was right," Longridge said to his friend. "The animals *are* traveling west along the line of my map. The little girl, Helvi Nurmi, looked after Tao for a short time. And a man saw two dogs in the Ironmouth mountains. And a farmer saw an old white dog who was stealing one of his chickens!"

Peter smiled for the first time when he heard this. He could see Bodger enjoying himself in a fight. But he knew that his old dog was really dead. And Luath.

Elizabeth was different from her brother. She was sure that Tao was alive. "He'll come home soon," she told her family. "I don't believe that he's dead. You'll see."

But only Elizabeth was hopeful. Longridge and the rest of the Hunter family looked at the map: the animals were in wild, lonely country.

"They can't be alive now," Jim Hunter told his family sadly. "But I hope their incredible journey ended quickly and without pain."

◆

Some weeks later, Longridge visited the Hunters again. People continued to ring about the animals, but there was no good news. It was Peter's twelfth birthday the following Sunday.

"Let's all go to Lake Windigo for a short vacation," Longridge suggested to the family.

"But maybe Tao will come back when we're away," said Elizabeth.

Longridge showed her Lake Windigo on the map. "It's on the line I drew," he told her.

Elizabeth agreed, full of hope. So they left for Lake Windigo to stay in the Hunters' small cabin there. It was almost winter and the lake was cold. There were no boats and all the other cabins were empty. Peter had a new camera and he went into the woods for hours with it. Elizabeth played in a treehouse near the lake.

On the last afternoon, the Sunday of Peter's birthday, they decided to go for a long walk. It was a beautiful, clear day and they walked in friendly silence. Each person was quietly thinking to himself. Jim Hunter missed his dog. He remembered walking with Luath on other fall days, gun in hand. And he remembered hunting with Luath on lakes, waiting patiently for hours in boats with him.

Peter remembered his last birthday as he walked up the hill. "Do you remember Bodger last year, Dad?" he asked his father. "I tried to teach him to hunt, but he didn't enjoy it. He soon got bored, poor old Bodger."

Peter suddenly felt very lonely and started crying quietly. But he didn't want his family to see, so he quickly picked up his camera.

They sat for a long time on the rocks at the top of the hill. It was very quiet. A bird sang and another bird ate some of their cookies. Everyone was silent and busy with their thoughts.

Suddenly, Elizabeth stood up.

"Listen!" she said. "Listen, Daddy! There's a dog barking!"

Everyone listened, but no one heard anything.

"You're imagining things," said her mother. "Or maybe it was another animal. We must go back now."

"Wait, wait! You'll hear it in a minute too," said Elizabeth quietly.

Her mother remembered that the child's hearing was still very good. She could hear noises that were lost to adults forever. And now even to Peter. So she stayed silent.

Elizabeth's excited, listening face changed to a huge smile. "It's Luath!" she said. "I know that bark!"

"Don't do this, Liz," said her father. "It's…"

Now Peter thought he heard something too. "*Shhh*!" he said to his father.

There was silence again as everyone listened hard. Jim Hunter felt strangely nervous. He got up and hurried down the hill with Peter behind him.

Then they both heard the bark. They stood there in the quiet afternoon, waiting to welcome an exhausted traveler. They didn't have to wait long.

A small body with a chocolate-colored tail came running through the trees on the high hillside. With a welcoming cry the Siamese jumped down the last two meters and landed at their feet. Elizabeth was smiling all over her face now. She got down on her knees and picked up the excited cat.

"Oh, Tao!" she said softly as she took him in her arms. He put his brown paws lovingly around her neck. "Tao!" she said again, kissing him. And Tao tightened his paws around her neck.

A second later, the Labrador arrived. He was much thinner and weaker than before, a shadow of the beautiful dog Longridge knew. He made excited noises as he jumped up to his master. When Longridge saw his friend Jim's face, he had to turn away.

Minutes passed. Everyone started talking excitedly at the same time. Luath barked and barked. He was shaking all over his body, and his eyes never left his master's face. The cat, on Elizabeth's shoulder, joined in with loud cries. Everyone laughed, talked, or cried at the same time. There was a lot of noise in the quiet wood!

Then, suddenly, there was silence. Everybody was thinking the same thought. No one looked at Peter. When Luath ran to him, he turned away.

"I'm glad he's back, Dad," he said. "And your Tao too!" he added to Elizabeth, with a difficult smile.

Elizabeth, usually the happy one, started to cry. Peter touched Tao behind the ears.

Everyone laughed, talked, or cried at the same time.

"You go back to the cabin," he said to his family. "I want to go up the hill to take a photo…"

"Shall I come too, Peter?" Longridge asked. And, to his surprise, the boy accepted his offer.

They watched the rest of the family walking down the hill. Tao lay in Elizabeth's arms and Luath walked close behind his master. Peter and Longridge returned to the top of the hill to take some photos. And all the time they talked. About everything, but not about dogs.

At last Longridge looked at his watch. It was time to go. He looked at Peter. "Let's…" he started to say. But he stopped when he saw the boy's excited face.

Down below, out of the darkness of the woods and into the light of the sun, came Bodger! Thin and tired, hopeful, happy—and hungry. Bodger, the dear old terrier, was coming as fast as he could!

He started to run, faster and faster, and threw himself at Peter. John Longridge turned away then and left them in the private world of boy and dog. He started walking toward the lake when he suddenly saw a small animal in front of him. It ran past his legs and its long tail disappeared up the hill in a second.

It was Tao, returning for his old friend. They were ending their incredible journey together.

ACTIVITIES

Chapters 1–3

Before you read

1 Read the Introduction to the book. Discuss these questions.
- **a** Why do you think the animals decide to go home?
- **b** How will they find food to eat on their journey?
- **c** How do you think their incredible journey will end?

2 Look at the Word List at the back of the book.
   Find:
- **a** two words for dogs
- **b** two words for wild animals
- **c** two words for people
- **d** one word for a building you can live in

While you read

3 Are these sentences right (✓) or wrong (✗)?
- **a** The three animals belong to the Hunters.   .....
- **b** Longridge takes the animals on vacation.   .....
- **c** Mrs. Oakes knows where the animals really are.   .....
- **d** The Labrador is a good hunter.   .....
- **e** The bears are afraid of the cat.   .....
- **f** Luath and Tao look after Bodger after his fight
        with the bear.   .....

After you read

4 Answer the questions.
- **a** Why are the animals living with Longridge?
- **b** Where does Longridge go on vacation? Who does he go with?
- **c** Where does Mrs. Oakes think the animals are? Why does she think this?
- **d** Which animal finds enough to eat on the journey?
- **e** What type of country do the animals travel through?
- **f** What attacks Bodger, the old white terrier?

5 Work with another student. Have this conversation.

Student A: You are Mrs. Oakes. You are telling your husband, Bert, about the animals. Tell him about the empty house and your search for the animals. Tell him where you think the animals are now.

Student B: You are Bert. Ask Mrs. Oakes questions about the animals. For example: What did Longridge say on the phone? Do you want me to call the police about the animals?

Chapters 4–7

Before you read

6 What do you think is the most dangerous thing for the animals on their journey? Is it too little food? Is it wild animals? Or are there other dangers?

7 Do you think Bodger, the terrier, will finish the journey and get home? Why (not)?

While you read

8 What happens first? Number these sentences 1–6.

a The Nurmi family look after the cat.   .....
b The dam on the stream breaks.   .....
c The Indians give the terrier and the cat food.   .....
d The Labrador cannot save the cat in the river.   .....
e An old man invites the animals to eat with him.   .....
f The old terrier swims across the river.   .....

After you read

9 Read these sentences. Which sentences are untrue? Correct them.

a The old terrier loves human beings.
b The Indians are unfriendly toward the animals.
c The animals have a good meal with the old man.
d The cat loves the water and swimming.
e Helvi has never had a pet before.
f When the cat lives with the Nurmis, he is deaf.

10 The Indians believe that the old dog will bring them luck in the future. Do you think that animals or other things can bring you luck? Or is it stupid to think like this?

Chapters 8–11

Before you read

11 Do you think the cat will find the two dogs again? Why?
12 How will Longridge and the Hunters feel when they find out about the lost animals?

While you read

13 Are these sentences right (✓) or wrong (✗)?
    a The two dogs steal a chicken.   .....
    b The cat kills a wild lynx.   .....
    c The Mackenzies look after both dogs.   .....
    d Longridge realizes that the animals are going
       home.   .....
    e Peter is more hopeful than Elizabeth about
       finding the animals.   .....
    f Bodger is the first to arrive home.   .....

After you read

14 Who says these words?
    a "He's an English bull terrier. I love them."
    b "I want them if they'll stay. But we must think of names for them."
    c "The animals have disappeared. But they were happy here. Why did they leave?"
    d "That Luath! Why did Bodger follow him to his death? And why didn't Tao stop Luath? Poor old Bodger."
    e "Listen! There's a dog barking!"
    f "I'm glad he's back...And your Tao too!"

15 Discuss this question. Do you think it is surprising that all the animals reach home alive? Why (not)?

Writing

16 You work for the newspaper *The Ontario News*. Write about the animals' journey for the newspaper. Write about the type of country they traveled through, two or three of their adventures, and the meeting between the Hunters and the animals at Lake Windigo.

17 Write the phone conversation between Longridge and Jim Hunter when Hunter comes home from England. Longridge has to tell him that the animals have disappeared. What does he say? And how does Hunter reply? What questions does he ask? What do they decide to do?

18 You are Elizabeth or Peter. Write a letter to a friend in England. Write about your return to Canada. How did you feel when your pet wasn't there? Did you think he was alive or dead? And how did you feel when you found your pet?

19 You are Helvi, the little girl who found Tao. Write about your days and nights at home with your new pet. How did you feel when you found the cat? What did your father do to make him better? What did you do with the cat every afternoon when you got back from school? How do you feel now?

WORD LIST

bark (v) when a dog barks, it makes short, loud sounds

bear (n) a large, strong animal that lives in forests

bull terrier (n) a small, strong type of dog

cabin (n) a small house made of wood, usually in the forest or mountains

curious (adj) wanting to know or learn about something

dam (n) a wall built across a river, by men and sometimes by animals, to stop the water

deaf (adj) unable to hear

exhausted (adj) very tired

huge (adj) very large

human being (n) a man, woman, or child

hunt (v) to catch and kill animals

incredible (adj) so strange that you cannot believe it

journey (n) a long trip from one place to another

Labrador retriever (n) a large dog. Labradors often guide people who cannot see.

leaf (n) one of the flat, green parts of a plant or tree

lynx (n) a large, wild cat

master (n) the man who owns an animal

paw (n) the foot of an animal, for example a cat or a dog

struggle (v) to try hard for a long time to do something difficult

wag (v) when a dog wags its tail, it moves its tail from one side to another

MOST POPULAR
PENGUIN READERS

AT LEVEL 3

The Adventures of Huckleberry Finn

The Beatles

The Black Cat and Other Stories

Braveheart

Forrest Gump

Martin Luther King

Matilda

Rain Man

Romeo and Juliet

Silas Marner

Stories from Shakespeare

Striker